MW00964746

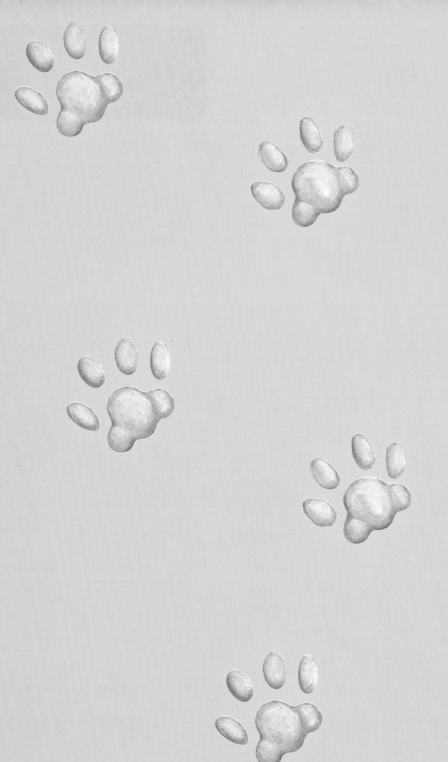

Minnie Kitten has a Bad Day

For Catrin

HAPPY CAT BOOKS

Published by Happy Cat Books Ltd.
Bradfield, Essex CO11 2UT, UK

First published 2003
1 3 5 7 9 10 8 6 4 2

Text and illustrations copyright © Michèle Coxon 1999, 2003

A CIP catalogue record for this book is available from the British Library

ISBN 1 903285 60 7

Printed in Poland

Minnie Kitten has a Bad Day

Happy Cat Books

Minnie kitten was climbing up the table-cloth.

"Get down Minnie!" called her mother. "You'll pull everything off!"

"I'm going out to play," muttered Minnie.

"Good idea," said her mother, "and don't get into trouble."

Out on the doorstep was a baby robin. "Hmmm," whispered Minnie, "I could just about catch you."

"Leave me alone, you big bully!" cheeped the little bird. "My mum and dad will be back soon and they'll peck your nose off."

Sure enough, in a moment the two robins flew back.

"Go away, you horrible kitten," they squawked as they pecked at Minnie's shiny fur.

Minnie crept into the barn. Bella the calf was there, drinking from a big bucket.

"Hello, Bella," mewed Minnie. "What have you got in there?"

"Careful, Minnie!" mooed Bella softly. "Don't knock it over."

Splash! Fresh milk poured over everything. Minnie lapped at it for a while.

"Well, there's too much milk here for me," she thought and she marched off to check on the hens.

The hens weren't there, but their eggs were.

"This is fun," purred Minnie, as she pedalled her furry paws against each egg.

"Cluck, cluck, cluck!" called an angry hen.
"Stop spoiling my eggs, you silly kitten."

Minnie slipped away feeling unwanted.

Usually, Monty the puppy chased Minnie, but today he was snoring in his bed.

"Oh look!" mewed Minnie. "Monty's favourite ball!"

Bang! The ball burst in Minnie's face.

"I think my claws are too sharp to play with it. I hope Monty won't be cross with me."

Ellie, the baby donkey, was resting under the apple tree.

"Look at those funny long ears!" thought Minnie. "I'll just give them a little pat."

She leaned down from the branch.

"Eee-Aaaaw!" brayed Ellie's mum. "Go away and find someone else to play with."

"Well," said Minnie, "you've certainly got long ears and very big teeth!" And she ran off.

Barney the piglet was in his sty. Minnie nipped his curly tail with her sharp little teeth.

"I've got you!" she laughed. "You can't get away now."

Mummy pig came thundering along. "Grunt, grunt!" she snorted. "You naughty kitten! I'll bite your tail."

"Oh no, you won't!" squeaked Minnie, and away she ran.

In the garden was a tiny mouse. Minnie kept
very still. She bent down very low in the grass.
"I can catch it. I can catch it," she whispered.

Suddenly, the mouse saw Minnie. It leapt up and bit her hard on the nose.

"Ouch!" yelped Minnie. "That hurt! I'm going back to my mum."

Mum was very pleased to see Minnie. "Where have you been all day?" she asked. "Have you had fun?"

"Lots of fun," purred Minnie,
"and I wasn't naughty once!"

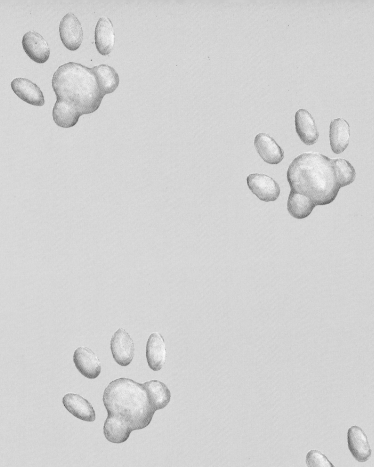